Welcome to Percy's Park!

Percy the park keeper works hard looking after the park and his animal friends who live there. But Percy still likes to find time for some fun and games. And, of course, in Percy's Park, there's always time for a story…

The Secret Path

First published in hardback in Great Britain by HarperCollins*Publishers* Ltd in 1994
First published in paperback by Picture Lions in 1995
New editions published by Collins Picture Books in 2003 and HarperCollins *Children's Books* in 2011 and 2019
This edition published as part of a set in 2018 and 2020

27 29 30 28

ISBN: 978-0-00-715518-7

Picture Lions and Collins Picture Books are imprints of the Children's Division, part of HarperCollins*Publishers* Ltd.
HarperCollins *Children's Books* is a division of HarperCollins*Publishers* Ltd.

Text and illustrations copyright © Nick Butterworth 1994, 2011, 2019

Visit our website at: www.harpercollins.co.uk

Printed in China

Nick Butterworth
The Secret Path

HarperCollins *Children's Books*

In leafy green hedges,
 the doorway was wide.
You looked and you wondered
 and then stepped inside.
The puzzling pathways
 took you along,
A turn to the right
 turned out to be wrong.
But when all that seemed left
 turned out to be right,
You entered the centre,
 a wonderful sight!
But now comes the hard part,
 to find the right track,
To retrace your steps;
 the secret path back.
The maze is a trickster,
 of that there's no doubt.
The maze let you in,
 but it won't let you out!

"I know. It's a shame," said Percy the park keeper to his small friend.

Percy had been looking after a young squirrel who had fallen out of a tree and hurt his arm.

"And I bumped my nose on Thursday," went on the squirrel.

"Mmm, I see," said Percy, who was not really giving the squirrel his full attention.

Percy was busy searching for something.

"Aha! Here it is," said Percy. "String. We'll need this today."

As Percy and the squirrel trundled their way across the park, they didn't notice a group of friends hiding behind a large tree.

"I've been meaning to fix up the old maze for ages," said Percy. "The hedges are terribly overgrown."

"Percy's going to work on the maze," said the fox.

"Let's race him there and have some fun!" said the badger, and he began to whisper excitedly.

The others squeaked with delight as they listened. Only the hedgehog wasn't so sure. He found the maze rather confusing.

"I don't think I'll come," he said. "I've…er… got something to do."

Percy parked his wheelbarrow by the entrance to the maze.

"Aren't you worried about getting lost in the maze?" the squirrel asked.

"That's why I need the string," said Percy. "I leave a trail of string from where I'm working back to the entrance of the maze. That way, I can't get lost, you see?"

The squirrel didn't really see because he wasn't really listening.

"I'm not sure if I like spring or autumn the best," he said.

At the back of the maze, a line of animals was disappearing one by one into the thick hedge.

"We'll go right to the middle and wait for Percy," whispered the badger.

"Then we'll jump out and give him a big surprise," giggled the rabbits.

"Ssshh!" said the fox loudly, which set them all giggling again.

ercy worked hard with his hedge clippers and little by little the maze began to look much tidier. All the time, Percy followed his string in and out of the maze.

By now, the surprise party had made its way
to the centre of the maze, where there stood
a stone bench. The bench had been carved to look
like a lion.

At first the animals waited eagerly for Percy to
come. But Percy took longer than they expected.
Soon they began to yawn. Then they fell asleep.

Percy's hedge clippers clacked on and on,
only stopping now and then when Percy
went to dump a barrow load
of clippings.

As Percy pushed his empty wheelbarrow back towards the maze, a hedgehog called to him.

"Hello Percy. Did you get a big surprise from the animals in the maze?"

"A big surprise?" Percy stopped and smiled. "Er…not yet," he said.

When at last Percy and the squirrel worked their way to the centre of the maze, there was no big surprise waiting for them.

Percy chuckled at the sight of the sleeping animals in front of him.

"Let's have some fun ourselves," he whispered.

Percy tiptoed to the back of the lion-shaped bench and coughed loudly.

"Ahem. I beg your pardon," said Percy in a deep, growly voice.

The fox opened one eye.

"It's not that I mind so very much," went on
    Percy, "but I do like people to ask before they
go to sleep on me."

The other animals began to stir.

The fox stared at the lion's head.

He couldn't believe
his ears.

"I'm very sorry," said the fox. "We didn't realise.
We thought you were just a seat."
The other animals opened their eyes in
amazement to hear the fox talking to a lump of
stone. They were even more
amazed when the stone
answered back.

"Did you indeed?" said
the growly voice.
"Just a seat.
Hmm."

"We're very sorry," said the fox. "Will you tell us your name?"

Percy growled. "My name is…"

But at that moment, one of the rabbits looked behind the bench.

"His name is Percy!" cried the rabbit.

The game was up and a chuckling Percy came out from behind the bench.

"Percy's tricked us, instead!" said the badger.

The fox suddenly started to giggle. That set everybody else giggling again.

"Come on," said Percy, as he collected his tools together, "who'd like toasted teacakes for tea? I'll show you the way out of the maze. All we have to do is to follow my str…"

But Percy didn't finish. Standing there in front of him, was his little squirrel helper. The squirrel was holding a large ball of string.

"Don't forget this, Percy," he said. "I've wound it all up for you."

Percy looked dismayed.

"Don't worry," said the fox, "I think this is the way out."

"No, no," said the badger. "I'm sure it's this way."

"Surely it's this way," said another voice.

"I might be wrong," said the squirrel holding the ball of string, "but I've got a feeling it's this way."

Percy groaned.

"And I've got a feeling we'll be having toasted teacakes for breakfast!"

"I was born in London in 1946 and grew up in a sweet shop in Essex. For several years I worked as a graphic designer, but in 1980 I decided to concentrate on writing and illustrating books for children.

My wife, Annette, and I have a son, Ben, and a daughter, Amanda, and three wonderful grandchildren.

I haven't recently counted how many books there are with my name on the cover but Percy the Park Keeper accounts for a good many of them. I'm reliably informed that they have sold in their millions worldwide. Hooray!

I didn't realise this when I invented Percy, but I can now see that he's very like my mum's dad, my grandpa. Here's a picture of him giving a ride to my mum and my brother, Mike, in his old home-made wheelbarrow!"

Nick Butterworth has presented children's stories on television, worked on a strip for *Sunday Express Magazine* and worked for various major graphic design companies. Among his books published by HarperCollins are *Thud!, QPootle5, Jingle Bells, Albert le Blanc, Tiger* and *The Whisperer,* which won the Nestlé Gold Award. But he is best known for his stories about Percy the Park Keeper, which have sold more than nine million copies worldwide. Percy has also appeared in his own television series.

Look out for more Percy the Park Keeper stories
OVER 9 MILLION COPIES SOLD!

PB: 978-0-00-714693-2

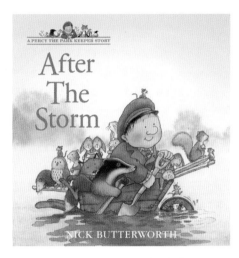

PB: 978-0-00-715515-6

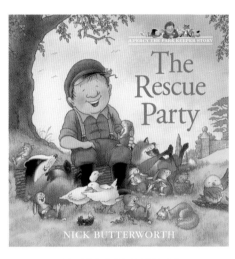

PB: 978-0-00-715516-3

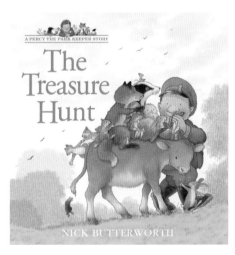

PB: 978-0-00-715517-0

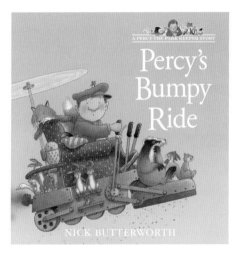

PB: 978-0-00-715514-9

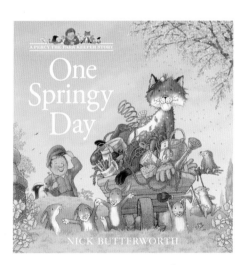

HB: 978-0-00-827986-8
PB: 978-0-00-827989-9

Percy the Park Keeper stories can be ordered at:
www.harpercollins.co.uk